Hedgehog's 100th Day of School

By Lynne Marie
Illustrated by Lorna Hussey

Scholastic Inc.

D0473857

Text copyright © 2017 by Lynne Marie
Illustrations copyright © 2017 by Lorna Hussey
Photos ©: 32: subjug/iStockphoto.

All rights reserved. Published by Scholastic Inc., *Publishers since 1920.*
SCHOLASTIC and associated logos are trademarks and/or registered trademarks
of Scholastic Inc.

The publisher does not have any control over and does not assume any
responsibility for author or third-party websites or their content.

No part of this publication may be reproduced, stored in a retrieval system, or
transmitted in any form or by any means, electronic, mechanical, photocopying,
recording, or otherwise, without written permission of the publisher. For
information regarding permission, write to Scholastic Inc., Attention: Permissions
Department, 557 Broadway, New York, NY 10012.

This book is a work of fiction. Names, characters, places, and incidents are
either the product of the author's imagination or are used fictiously, and any
resemblance to actual persons, living or dead, business establishments, events,
or locales is entirely coincidental.

ISBN 978-1-338-11309-9

10 9 8 7 6 5 4 3 2 1   17 18 19 20 21

Printed in the U.S.A.   40
First printing 2017
Book design by Lizzy Yoder

To Kevin and Kayla because I can easily
think of at least 100 ways in which I love
each of you, and to Valeria, Sofia, and
Salvatore for the more than 100 days of
sunshine they have brought to our lives.
—L.M.

For Sue
My amazing high school teacher
With love and thanks
—L.H.

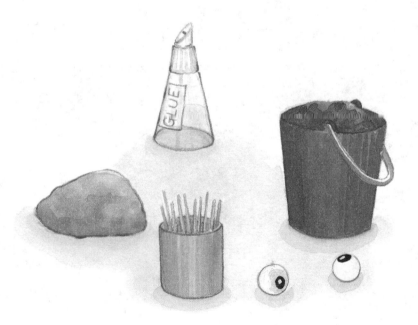

Spike clutched his homework. "This is Miss Moose's best assignment ever!" he said. "We get to make an art project and march in a parade to celebrate the 100th day of school!"

He couldn't wait to tell Mama Hedgehog.

Spike listened to his classmates chatter about their project ideas.

"I'll glue 99 paper lily pads with flowers to a board," Lily announced. "Then I'll add one plastic frog to make 100."

"Paper flowers?" Wart croaked. "How boring. I'm bringing 100 flies stuck to flypaper."
Lily stuck out her tongue.

"I'm going to wear a cardboard crown with 100 gems," bragged King. "Then I'll lead the parade and rule the school!"

"Well, I'm bringing 100 shells from my collection," said Sheldon. "What about you, Spike?"

Spike realized he didn't have an idea for his project! He sighed. "I'm not sure yet."

Spike raced home, waving his homework. "Look, Mama!"

Mama read every word. "This sounds like a fun project, Spike. What will you make?"

Spike hung his head. "Everyone else thought of perfect ideas, but I don't know where to start."

"Look inside yourself," Mama suggested.

Spike looked inside himself. He didn't see anything but teeth and a tongue.

"Give yourself time," said Mama.

Spike stood on his head
and rolled into a ball.

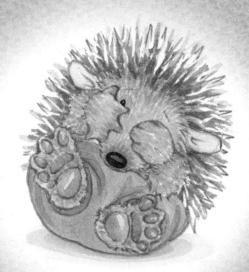

No ideas came.

"I'll take a walk," he said.
"Mind your quills," said Mama.

Spike spotted Hoot outside his tree house, gluing 50 pairs of googly eyes onto a circle.

"What a great idea for your project," said Spike. "I'm still stumped."

"Take a pair of eyes," said Hoot.
Spike slipped them into his pocket and said
good-bye to his friend.

Next, Spike came across Hopper in his carrot garden, where he was arranging stones. "What's your 100th-day project?" Spike asked.

"A snapshot of my rock sculpture. What's yours?"

"The seeds of my idea haven't sprouted yet," Spike admitted.

Hopper counted his rocks: "99, 100, 101! Oops!" He handed Spike the extra stone.

"Here's something for *your* project."

"Thanks," said Spike.

Spike wandered past the pond and noticed Wade pouring a thick mixture into a pail. "It's sand clay," Wade explained as he stuck 100 umbrellas in the mold.

"That's just right for a flamingo," remarked Spike.

Wade offered Spike a second pail of clay. "Mold it into something for *your* project."
  "Thanks," said Spike.

Farther along, Spike met Sticks, who was carefully placing one last toothpick atop his miniature dam. "Nice job!" said Spike.

Sticks scratched his head. "Why aren't you home working on your project?"

Spike looked at the ground. "I don't have an idea yet."

"But you have supplies." He handed Spike his box of extra toothpicks.

Spike studied the objects his friends had given him: a pair of googly eyes, a rock, a pail of clay, and a box of toothpicks. He thought about what his mama had said. *Look inside yourself. Mind your quills.*

Then he put it ALL together.

Spike raced home, rushing past Mama at the front door. "I know what to do!"

On the 100th day of school, Spike listened to his classmates present their projects.

"It's your turn to present, Spike," said Miss Moose.

Spike cradled a clay-covered rock hedgehog with two googly eyes. 100 toothpicks stuck out from the clay.

"I was really stumped about what to make," Spike explained, "but each of my friends gave me supplies. Then I figured out how to put them all together."

"That's a great project, Spike. I'm glad you didn't give up," said Miss Moose. Spike smiled proudly.

And when the class marched in their 100th Day of School Project parade, who do you think led the line?

HEDGEHOG'S 100TH DAY OF SCHOOL

Do you need an idea for your 100th-day project?
Here's a list of fun ways Spike's classmates
made their 100th day special!

- Snap the Alligator drew pictures of 100 of her favorite things.

- Hue the Chameleon glued 100 crayons
onto a poster board to look like a rainbow.

- Kailani the Hawaiian Goose made a lei
(flower necklace) with 100 flowers.

- Hera the Horned Owl wrote a list of 100 of her favorite words.

- Hazel the Mouse cut out pictures of 100 of her favorite cheeses.

- Muck and Myra Pig gathered 100 recyclable items.

- Peek-a-Boo the Ostrich buried 100 prizes in a box of sand.
Each of her friends got to dig for the prizes!

- Romeo the Rat picked 100 ivy leaves
to add to a picture he drew of Rapunzel in her tower.

- Sheldon the Turtle dressed up as a 100-year-old turtle.

- Stripes the Zebra collected 100 black
and white buttons in a jar.

Now it's your turn—what will
you do for your 100th day?